The Crockett Tales
for Children

Tilly Crockett

authorHOUSE®

AuthorHouse™ UK Ltd.
500 Avebury Boulevard
Central Milton Keynes, MK9 2BE
www.authorhouse.co.uk
Phone: 08001974150

First published by AuthorHouse 5/27/2009

ISBN: 978-1-4389-6154-5 (sc)

Printed in the United States of America
Bloomington, Indiana

This book is printed on acid-free paper.

THE CROCKETT TALES are short stories for children which emphasise the importance of kindness to people and animals and the protection of our environment. The virtues of patience, obedience, honesty, kindness and wisdom are recurring themes. There are ten entertaining short stories with lively illustrations. All convey in an interesting way a moral which even young children can understand. Children need to respect themselves, others, animals and the environment. All of us need to be less self-seeking, less money-conscious and to be more patient with relatives and friends. The Crockett tales project a new message with each story and allow the reader to think about his own way of improving society.

These stories have been inspired by Billy Crockett and written by Tilly Crockett

Illustrations by Milly Crockett.

Contents

SOOTY THE DOG MAKES A DECISION

Imagine my surprise on returning home from school to find a small dog curled up on the doormat. "Hello" I said calmly as he looked at me with some suspicion. He hastily moved aside but he did not refuse my invitation to come inside. His tail started wagging and I think that he smiled at me! He was a young male dog about three months old. Although bedraggled and muddied, he was a real beauty. He had charcoal-coloured hair with soft curls on top of his head. "Mum" I called, "Come and see our visitor". Mum was busy in the kitchen but the mention of a visitor roused her curiosity. "Oh, what a lovely dog", said Mum. "But to whom does he belong"? she added.

"I found him here on the mat" I replied. "Can he stay while we look for his owner"? I asked as the dog jumped up on the sofa and started to scratch himself! "Well" replied mum, "I do not think that I can send him home right now because he may not have a home". I knew that mum loved dogs and would for the moment anyhow agree to let him in, in spite of the fleas!

The dog was by now inspecting all corners of the room. With a knowing grin, mum suggested that he might like to visit the back garden before supper. He wagged his tail and off he went, zigzagging excitedly through the grass. We watched from the kitchen window as he disappeared behind the ash trees. A short time later he seemed to be taken by surprise by a ginger cat sitting on the garden wall who hissed at him, causing him to beat a quick retreat to the kitchen door! We had no meat in the house. Mum suggested that the dog might like some bread and scrambled eggs. He ate the eggs and a little of the bread, wagged his tail, curled up on a woollen mat and fell asleep. Then mum phoned the Society for Prevention of Cruelty to Animals (SPCA), the local vet. and the police, enquiring if anyone had lost the little dog. Nobody had informed any of them regarding a missing pet.

The kind man from the SPCA shook his head and said. "Perhaps his owner has gone on holiday and forgotten about the dog. Dogs give us so much and ask very little in return. People need to remember that the dog is part of the family and needs to be looked after too"!

He was a well-mannered dog and in spite of his young age he did not touch anything apart from playing with some old stockings that I had rolled into a ball. He also liked tearing an old shoe that mum had given him. I noticed that he had some beautiful small teeth! Over the next few days we grew used to the dog who was no trouble at all as long as he had a walk or two and an old shoe! Luckily I loved walking too and found the time to take him at least a short distance, morning and evening. Mum often came too. I took him with me everywhere that I could but even when left alone for a few hours, he slept peacefully beside his shoe! Several weeks went by and nobody claimed him. I called him Pedro as he looked like a dog of that name, that I had seen in a magazine. I washed him and mum got him his vaccinations and anti-scabies and anti-flea shots from the local vet. The vet was impressed with how he stood and remained quiet while he received his injections. It was as if he knew that these would protect him.

Two weeks later as I walked with Pedro in a nearby park a little boy approached me. I thought that he was going to pat the dog and I was going to tell him to be careful. Nobody, not even a well-mannered and quiet dog, likes to be taken by surprise, because a hand, even a small hand can be threatening when you are not expecting this to come down on your head! However I was not prepared to hear the boy exclaim:

"That's my brother's dog. He is called Sooty. Sooty went missing when Joe got sick and had to go into hospital but he is better now. Come on, I'll show you". The little boy lead me to his home not too far away, where I heard shrieks of delight as Sooty was reunited with Joe. I was near to tears. I could not believe that I had grown so attached to the dog so quickly. He was a real charmer but unfortunately Pedro no longer existed. Sooty was not mine. I patted him gently as I gave Joe the new blue dog collar and lead that I had bought for him. As I walked away I could see Sooty looking sadly at me. While he was delighted to be back with his owner he seemed to want to say. "Thank you". Mum tried to console me. She missed Sooty but she was delighted that his owner had been reunited with him. She promised that in time we would visit the local dog shelter to see if I could get a dog of my very own.

Sooty paid us another visit. One day I heard a loud bark at the door and there he was. He bounded inside and promptly went to sleep on the sofa. I had not the heart to disturb him! When he awoke he let me pat him, rolled over, got up and shook the tiredness away as he approached the door. With a bound he skipped off down the path. As I watched from the window I noticed that he returned home through a narrow railing close-by. Over the next few days he called again and promptly hopped up on the sofa. I think he liked his owner's food, but preferred our sofa! The alternating lifestyle came to an end when we went away on holiday. On my return I heard that Sooty had got tangled in the wire separating our garden from the end of the laneway near his house. Although he was not hurt I think that he began to realise that it was far wiser to stay on his own side of the fence. I met Joe who said that Sooty now plays with him in his own garden. I still see Sooty occasionally, walking with Joe. He seems to know that he can only be faithful to one master and there is really no place like home!

CAROLINE'S AMAZING PICTURE

Caroline lived with her mother in a basement-room in a dingy narrow street in a large city. The room was humid and must-smelling in summer, and damp and draughty in winter.

Caroline's dad had been killed in a car accident when she was a baby. The accident had injured her mum. As a result her mother was not able to move about very quickly and she walked with a stick. Her mother was an honest hardworking woman but her lameness slowed her up a lot and because of this her weekly wage was not very big. When the rent was paid and the food for the week bought, there was little money left. They were poor but they were happy.

Caroline was seven but she was small and thin for her age. She had long brown hair and big blue eyes. She worked hard and came to school every day. She was a quiet silent girl but she always joined her school companions in their fun and laughter. Although she was reserved she had both a kindness and a refreshing honesty which made her popular with other pupils and the teachers.

Caroline had to walk through a number of narrow streets on her way to school. There were many small shops in those streets but Caroline never had money to spend. She passed them every day without taking much notice of the things that were for sale in them. There was however one shop which Caroline really liked. This shop was known as "The Treasure". Jake, the shop owner, was a tall bearded man who always seemed to be moving things in or out of the big window. There was one object in the shop window which fascinated Caroline. It was a picture of a little boy. His face was very round with rosy cheeks. The face was surrounded by fair curly hair. It reminded Caroline of the face of an angel that she had seen painted over the top of the Christmas crib. Caroline always thought that Angel smiled at her.

Every day on her way to school Caroline stood by the shop window. The little boy seemed to want to talk to her. At times Caroline even thought that his cheeks bulged in an effort to speak to her. When Caroline saw people going into the shop she shivered with fear in case they might buy the picture and take it away.

Caroline's eight birthday arrived and her mother gave her five Euro. It seemed such a lot to Caroline. Now her lucky day had arrived. She would try to buy the picture in Jake's shop. She went off to school early with her money carefully placed in her small purse, feeling very excited. On her way home she went into the shop to see Jake. " I want to buy the picture in the corner of the window", she said.

"Where is it"? he asked. Caroline quickly pointed it out to him.

"How much is it"? she asked.

"Oh" he said, "Show me how much money you have to spend". She showed him her money. He took the money, closed his hand and rubbed his nose with his closed fist. "You may as well have it", he said. Jake took the picture out, weighed it in his hand, looked at Caroline and asked her if she could carry it. Caroline took the picture and found it was indeed quite heavy. She was however determined to carry it home. The eyes of the Angel did seem to smile now. She arrived home at last and when her mother came in she met her at the door still holding the picture in her arms. Caroline was overjoyed with her birthday picture and her mother also admired the picture very much. Her mother said that it was a real oil painting!

The picture was placed on a shelf near the window where Caroline could see it every day. One Saturday afternoon as Caroline looked closely at the picture she thought that the whole round face seemed to bulge out from the rest of the head. There seemed to be a very faint line encircling the face, making it more prominent than the rest of the picture. The name of the painter was difficult to make out but two words looked like José and LeBrecht. Just then her mother entered the room and saw Caroline's intent face gazing at the picture. Her mother took the picture in her hands. Suddenly, out fell the face onto the table and from behind it fell an old yellow envelope. Caroline handed the envelope to her mother who opened it. There was a letter inside, dated 1887. It was a sad letter from the artist who had painted the picture. He, José LeBrecht had submitted the picture to an exhibition in Paris. The picture which was called 'The Cherub' had been rejected and the style of painting used by LeBrecht had been savagely criticized by the Board of the Academy. One of the sentences from the letter was deeply moving. "I seem to be a useless artist", wrote LeBrecht. "I must give away The Cherub. I may never paint again".

Caroline and her mother were in tears. To them at least, LeBrecht seemed such a powerful artist. 'The Cherub' had been so inspiring that Caroline wanted to talk to him every day. Caroline's mother briskly straightened up and said. "Never mind those critics. I am going to take the picture to the art teacher at your school. He is a fine teacher and he will know if the painting is good or not". Caroline sighed. She did not want to part with 'The Cherub' but she knew that her mother would take care of it.

Well the story has a happy ending. The art teacher was impressed by 'The Cherub' and told both Caroline and her mother that in his opinion the picture was worth quite a lot of money. He himself took the picture to a master art critic who agreed with him that the painting was valuable. The picture was repaired and the critic himself offered to buy the picture but Caroline refused to part with it. Instead she agreed to sell a copy of the picture with the letter from LeBrecht to the city art gallery. The letter was also extremely valuable because the art teacher explained to Caroline and her mother that LeBrecht had become famous and his pictures valuable only after his death. Before he died however he knew that many fellow artists admired his work. The letter would inspire all who despaired of becoming great artists, to keep on trying and to ignore destructive criticism. Caroline kept the picture in her bedroom where she could see and talk to 'The Cherub' every day. Caroline studied hard and became an art teacher. She helped many children to develop a love of art and to paint. She and her mother lived happily ever after.

PRITSIE THE WIND BABY

Pritsie Wind-Drop was a wind baby, who lived in a cloud faraway over the western sea in a place where the sun sinks in the evening. Her house was made of clouds, lovely white soft fleecy ones. Pritsie had a lot of fun dancing from one cloud to another and running up and down the fleecy stairs. Sometimes other wind children joined her in a game of hide and seek. When they played, the little clouds swayed backwards and forwards and shivered and shook and even changed their colour to black or dark navy as they danced.

When Pritsie wished to play on the ground she pushed a switch in the darkest cloud and the cloud stood on a mountain or hilltop. Then she raced up and down the mountain or hilltop and sometimes even dragged some of the little clouds with her along the hilltop or down the mountain slope. At other times she visited the villages and towns and tossed and ruffled the clothes on the clothes-lines and dried them all very quickly. Then busy earth mothers blessed and praised her. At other times however she behaved badly and blew dirt onto the clean white clothes and even squeezed water from one of the dark clouds onto them. Then the earth mothers were angry because their work was spoiled. When she grew tired, she pressed the cloud switch and soared in her cloud house back into the sky.

One day Pritsie got tired of playing in her cloud house. She ran round and round the hillside and soon other wind children joined her. They decided that it would be nice to have a dance together. They danced around the trees and set the leaves whispering. They hurled and buffeted the little birds about as they flew for shelter. They hummed as they jazzed and twisted to and fro. They got dizzy but the dizzier they grew the faster they spun until finally they rushed with a whining sound down into the valley below.

In the valley there was a small town with a row of beautiful wooden houses. Pritsie and her companions danced with great speed round and round the houses and tore off pieces of the roofs. Bits of clothing and children's toys could be seen all over the main street. Pritsie and her friends then flung the roof slates onto the street with great force, causing a poor old man to fall and hurt his leg. Then they snatched up many of the children's toys and threw them into the river where many sank to the bottom while others floated on the surface. A kind fisherman picked them up and brought them to the toy hospital. A toy doctor was called to the hospital immediately to repair the broken toys.

Pritsie and her companions danced and wheeled through the streets again, knocking down the sun shades from the windows and more slates from the roof-tops. Men, women and children as well as the birds and animals, ran for shelter as quickly as possible. Pritsie and her friends raced into the open countryside throwing down poles and uprooting trees and shrubs. Finally they came to the sea. It looked smooth, shiny and inviting like a prepared skating rink. "Let us dance on it", they all shouted together and off they ran onto the sea. Little boats and big boats scrambled out of their way. But some of the boats were not quick enough and they were kicked about and broken. The sailors found it difficult to save themselves. The wind children danced on and on, humming and whistling as they went. They danced all night and when morning came they grew tired. Some of them said that they would like to call on their friends in Africa and off they went. Others thought that it would be a good idea to go to the north pole and off they went. Pritsie was left alone, weary and forlorn. She stopped dancing and turned silently home where her mother was waiting for her. She looked sad and said to Pritsie. "You know you and your friends caused a lot of unhappiness and damage last night". Pritsie was ashamed because she had seen the damage that she and her friends had caused by acting so thoughtlessly. She promised that in future she would be careful how and where she played. Her mother reminded her that she must always be kind to others whether at work or at play. Then her mother wrapped her up gently in a nice white cloud and whispered to her.

"Having great power does not mean that you have to lose it. Remember Pritsie to use energy wisely".

WHY WE MUST ALL KEEP OUR PROMISES

In the beginning God made everything. He gave certain gifts or talents to each. He wanted everyone and everything to use those talents to do good to itself or to its neighbour and to give glory to God. When God had finished His work He asked each what they would do with their talents. He wanted to make sure that each understood what they should do. The Land said that it would do its best to feed God's people. The animals said that they would help man with his work and therefore help to feed and clothe him. The birds said that they would sing and try to make man happy. The Sun said that he would give light and heat and so help man in his work. The stars and the Moon said that they would light up at night and so remind man of God even in darkness. The Sea said. "I will try to feed many people of the world with my fish".

God on hearing all these intentions said. "These are all worthy promises however I have not created all of you just to serve mankind. Man must live and work with you all". God turned to man and asked: "You have a brain and freewill. What are you going to do to keep man and all animals in harmony with one another and the environment"?

Man replied. "I am going to populate the world with people who will be fed by the fish and other animals, serenaded by the birds, transported by the sea and air and illuminated by the stars, moon and sun".

God then asked: "How will you repay all the animals, the sea, the air and the environment for helping you to survive and populate"?

"I will look after the animals, the sea, the air and the environment", replied man.

"I will inspect your promises from time to time ", said God. "If these are not kept I will get angry, very angry", said God as he moved upwards into the heavens.

Time marched on. The animals, insects, birds, sea, moon and stars tried to keep their promises. From time to time there were lapses when animals behaved badly, the wind caused terrible damage, the sea moaned excessively and the sun's rays were too hot for the earth. However overall their promises were kept. The same cannot be said for man. Man has treated the animals cruelly and often makes them fight amongst themselves. He causes wars and kills other men. Man has damaged and polluted the sea and the wider environment. God is not pleased. From time to time He reminds man of his promises. Man however continues to damage the world. As the twenty-first century rolls on we must keep remembering to treat all men as equals, to treat all animals with respect and to thank God for our environment which we must value as a priceless inheritance. We must above all stop making God angry by making every effort to keep our promises.

JOE AND HIS ANIMAL FRIENDS

Joe was a travelling-man who carried all his possessions around with him in a cart. His cat Toast and his dog Rover travelled with him, usually at opposite ends of the cart which was pulled by a beautiful dark-brown horse called Mighty. Joe was an honest sort of fellow and he loved Mighty, Toast and Rover. He travelled from place to place because he liked to travel. He had a limp from birth so he carried a long stick to help him get on and off the cart. He called at all the houses as he went along the road, often working for the local farmers in the haymaking season. They paid him with their produce. He got potatoes, oatmeal, eggs or a piece of bacon carved from the fletches of the unfortunate pigs that he usually spotted in the farmyard on his previous round. He hated when the pigs got killed although he knew that the farmer had them killed without cruelty. He liked the bacon though and thanked the farmer's wife many times after receiving it.

All these goodies went into a long rucksack which he kept well away from Rover, in the middle of the cart. Sometimes he did not like carrying foodstuffs so he collected old clothes. He sold these to a factory which made paper.

Joe was a happy man. He never worried too much about tomorrow but he was getting older and he wondered if he could settle down somewhere with his three loyal friends Mighty, Toast and Rover. One day as he approached a small midland town he met the local postman who greeted him with great enthusiasm. "Joe, I am so glad to see you", he said. "I have a letter for you", he added. Joe was shocked. He had never received a letter before. In fact he was ashamed to admit that he could not read. He had never attended school so he was not able to read the daily paper, something he regretted as he often found that he missed important news. "Read me the letter please Tom", he said to the postman. Tom read the letter slowly while Joe listened intently. It was an important letter, informing Joe that the local council had given him a small cottage on an acre of ground just outside the town. Joe was speechless with delight. "Thanks Tom for your help" he said as he got back in the cart clutching his letter. He drove off to inspect his new home. With the help of some friendly neighbours Joe was able to move into his own cottage. A fire was lit in the cosy kitchen where Joe could stay warm and cook his food.

Mighty looked pleased as he started to eat the lush green grass. There was some rivalry though between Toast and Rover and they started to quarrel. Toast wanted to sit at the fire. Rover however felt that he should sit by Joe's feet in order to guard his master. After much barking and mewing it was decided how they would settle the matter. They should run a race and whichever of them would reach the back door first, well he could sit with Joe by the fire, while the loser would have to guard the house by watching everything that happened in the garden. Now the dog was pleased and happy as he knew that he could run faster than the cat and he was sure that he would win. They fixed the time and place and all the rules of the race were observed. They got ready while the neighbouring cats and dogs counted one, two and three and away they went.

The dog ran and ran and arrived at the back door in record time but who should be there but Joe. Joe had just been telling Mighty not to eat his neighbour's trees which were overhanging the garden. Mighty was not inclined to listen as some juicy green leaves which he liked were peeping over the fence just within his reach. Joe had to tell Mighty a couple of times to go back and eat the grass in the middle of his own garden before Mighty finally gave up on the neighbouring branches. After all the exertion Joe's leg started to ache and he needed to collect his stick from the cart. Joe emerged from the cart with his stick just as Rover came running by. Rover was sweating with his tongue hanging out as the sun was hot but he was determined to get to the back door and stake his claim to a place in the house. "Rover my boy whatever is the matter with you"? cried Joe, totally unaware of the contest between Toast and Rover as the dog tried to jump over and under, up and down and around the stick. After some time Toast came along hopping warily on his paws. He skipped gently and silently past Joe and Rover, ran inside the house and sat in the corner. Then he washed his face and smoothed down his whiskers and waited. "Rover may be fast but I am smarter"! he thought.

Joe patted Rover and hurried out to fetch some eggs, not realizing that he had unknowingly biased the contest in favour of Toast. Poor Rover. He rushed in to the house. There sat Toast purring happily. "Oh" said Toast. "You can look after the house on the outside but I got in before you and therefore I must stay inside and purr over everyone". Rover rushed at him calling "Cheat"! Toast jumped up on a chair. At that moment in came Joe. "You are acting very strangely Rover", said Joe as he added. "You are a big boy now, behave yourself"! Joe may not have known about the racing contest between Rover and Toast but he soon noticed that Rover was spending a lot of time in the garden, guarding the cottage. One day Rover found a lovely warm wooden kennel which Joe had made for him. It was placed underneath the old oak tree. It gave him the perfect view of both the garden and the house. Even more important, if Toast got too bossy Rover could always chase him up the tree!

Joe and the animals have learned to live in harmony again although Rover seldom gets too close to the fire. On occasions this is all too much for him so every time Joe is busy he gets an opportunity to rush after the cat hissing, "Cheat, cheat"! Toast is the picture of serenity and barely arches his back as he replies. "Who's a smart boy then"? Rover occasionally chases Toast up the tree but with Joe around this does not happen too often!

THE LITTLE DAISY

It was early one June morning. The sun was not long up and had not yet heated its rays too strongly. The dew shone like millions of diamonds on the grass, on the leaves of trees, on the flowers and particularly on the spiders' webs which hung in corners and under the big leaves of garden plants.

Craig the gardener lit his pipe and walked slowly along the garden path. Many sounds reached his ears, the baby chatter of young birds, the dreamy bleat of a young lamb, the buzz of a bee and the low hum of insects. Suddenly he thought that he heard voices. "Could it be the flowers in conversation"? he murmured to himself.

"Oh dear", said the rose as she pouted her scarlet leaves towards the sun, leaves which held a few large diamond-like tears of dew. "I give my perfume to the world but few appreciate my smell, my colour, my shape and my total beauty. I am sad and I feel humiliated when I see who has invaded my territory".

"What is troubling you my friend", said the tall lily with a puzzled pale expression.

"Oh" said the rose, "I am humbled to have to live side by side with such lowly creatures".

"I do not understand you", said the lily, as she stretched her neck and opened her snow-white satin leaves with a ladylike sweep. The rose replied. "You I do not resent, as after all you are elegant and beautiful but look at what has happened to me". As she spoke the rose looked around and said in a scornful voice. "What a plain creature now stands close to me". Her gaze was directed towards the small daisy who stood apart, shy and unassuming and at that moment gave her diamond dew drops generously to a small thirsty bird.

The lily's eyes were directed by the rose to the daisy and she listened intently while the rose spoke.

"Oh", said the lily, " I do not know why you talk like this, after all I heard the gardener say as he walked around the garden and saw the daisy".

"Oh daisy you are small but beautiful. Spring is indeed here. You are a ray of hope for all men". The lily continued to praise the daisy with whom she got on well and she added.

"The gardener's wife loves the daisy. She says that it reminds her of her national flag because the daisy is dressed in green, white and gold. I heard her saying to the daisy that it should be proud to carry such colours, that it was a great privilege to do so, a privilege denied to other flowers. When the gardener came to my bed he looked and wondered if I had the strength to survive at all and he looked at you my friend Rose and said thoughtfully to himself".

"I am afraid that the frost may destroy all your petals this year".

The lily uttered a final word of warning to the rose. "Be careful my beautiful Rose as your perfume may be a bit too strong, your nails too sharp and your colours too bright. Let us not scorn plain humble folk too much".

Days went by and the rose had to endure her humiliation until one day a small dog knocked some petals off and a slug crept into the remaining petals, curled himself up and remained there in spite of Rose's protests. Soon the colours of the petals faded. Earwigs settled in the lily's house and caused the beautiful white satin leaves to turn yellow and crumple up like withered paper. The daisy however smiled and did not complain about the dog, the slug or the earwig. The birds and the butterflies flew low to say "Hello" now and again, and the daisy was happy and contented. "I may be small but I am well-marked. The birds can see my water-drops, the bees can smell the pollen and Meg the gardener's wife likes my colours. I am so happy to be here with you all", she murmured as evening approached.

JACK THE UNFORTUNATE MOUSE

Jack was a lovable but greedy mouse. He would creep through the small pipe that led from the garden into Mrs Richards' kitchen and forage for crumbs, cheese or bacon rind. Mrs Richards was short-sighted and although she was house-proud she often did not see the small lumps of food which often got tossed onto the floor, behind the fridge, under the cooker and under the doormat. Josie, Jack's mother often warned Jack to stay away from the kitchen. She was slim, tidy and kept her house by the side of the oak-tree, spotless. She insisted that all the family eat natural products found as near as possible to the dwelling. "Jack", she said, "If you keep eating those big chunks of cheese and bacon you will get fat". Jack paid no heed. Initially he shared whatever he found in Mrs Richards' kitchen with his sisters and brothers, a fact to which Josie turned a blind eye because each only got a small portion. Soon however Jack got greedy and kept all the food for himself.   He spent all day in Mrs Richards' kitchen, leaving only for Josie's suppers which he ate as well as all the food that strayed into his path.

Mrs Richards was puzzled. "My, my, the floor is looking rather mottled with all those grains of black rice or are those seeds from the geranium on the sill"? Now unfortunately Mrs Richards was deluding herself. Those seeds were Jack's business cards which he left when he came calling!

Jack got bigger and bigger. One day he tumbled into the swing bin where Mrs Richards collected her thrash. He was so fat he could not climb out. Josie sent the rescue mice to find him. Alas, he was so heavy that George, Ginger, Moss and Pete between them could not lift him out of the bin. Jack had even eaten the thrash and had become very thirsty. "At least get me some of my mum's berry-juice", he cried through parched lips. The others exchanged glances. "Its not berries you need Jack", said Moss, "Its a trolley to the hospital". With that, all four lined up together in the bin and tilted it so that Jack could slide out. After six attempts, Jack started sliding but instead of sliding down and out, he fell on top of all four, hitting his head and theirs. There was a deadly silence as Mrs Richards came quickly into the kitchen. "I thought that something had fallen", she sighed as she turned the bin back to its upright position. Jack and his helpers have not been seen since.

THE BUCKLED SHOES

"They're lovely", shrieked Suzie as she gazed at the most beautiful pair of shoes imaginable. They were small shiny black patent leather pumps with the most exquisite gold buckles which glinted and gleamed in the pale moonlight. Suzie was on her way to the kitchen for a glass of milk when she spotted the shoes at the bottom of the back staircase. It was nearly midnight and way past her bed-time but the salty bacon sandwich from the night before had made her thirsty. She must stop using too much salt! Her thirst momentarily forgotten, she gazed at the shoes. "Mum must have bought these for my birthday", she thought as she reached out to touch one of the shoes. "Hey, steady on, I have just made those" said a shrill male voice which seemed to come from below the stairs. Suzie looked around but could see no one. She hesitated, remembering her parents' advice that she must not talk to strangers or indeed trust anyone who was acting strangely. Surely there was something very strange about someone who made shoes in the middle of the night in someone else's house?

"Who are you and why are you in my house"? she cried in a trembling voice, still unable to see anyone. "I'm here", said the voice again but this time it sounded nearer.
Suddenly there was a whistling sound and Suzie saw a small figure landing on the top step of the stairs. It was like a perfectly proportioned doll but it was alive and acrobatic. With a bow the figure straightened up and looked in Suzie's direction.   He was clad in a green jacket, black trousers and a red hat. He was red- complexioned and had a small pointed beard.
"Hello, I'm Hughie", he said. Suzie was for once almost speechless.
"I am Suzie", she managed to reply. "Did you make these beautiful shoes"?
"I did indeed", Hughie replied.
"May I try them on"? Suzie asked.
"No, they are mine". Hughie replied, pointing to his bare feet. "Anyhow, your feet are too big for the shoes". Suzie's lower lip trembled. Not only was she disappointed that the shoes were not for her but to be told that her feet were big, well that was real cheek! Hughie slipped into the patent shoes and suddenly began to dance. Suzie, forgetting her disappointment, watched as the shiny shoes and gleaming buckles sped across the small wooden floor at the top of the stairs. Hughie could dance and he did dance for what seemed a long time. As he pirouetted around the floor with a flamenco-style flourish he looked at her and smiled. "Be patient and you may soon get a pair of shoes like mine".
Suddenly Suzie heard her mother call her.
"Suzie, why are you sitting on the stairs", cried her mum.

"I am watching the dance", replied Suzie.

"What dance" said her mother who looked puzzled and half-asleep. Suzie started to explain but suddenly she noticed that Hughie had stopped dancing. He had suddenly disappeared.

"Suzie, I think that you are tired", said her mother. "Come to bed and let's talk about this tomorrow".

Suddenly Suzie felt very tired. She nodded off as soon as her head touched the pillow. The following day her mother greeted her with a smile. As she opened the curtains Suzie could see that her mother had a shoe-box in her hand. "I know that you wanted dancing shoes for your birthday Suzie. I think that you will like these", she added as she opened a black velvet box. Suzie held her breath as she slipped on a pair of shiny black patent leather pumps with exquisite gold buckles. These were a perfect fit.

THE RAINBOW

James was speechless. He and his friend Richard had been playing near the old yew tree at the back of Rainbow Mountain in Castletown when they heard the sound of singing and digging. Richard claimed to see a short man with a red hat and yellow trousers digging in the cluster of trees nearby. James saw nobody but could clearly hear singing. It went as follows: "I am a lucky man with a good heart, gold in a can and strong muscles for a wee man". James and Richard approached the trees as the singing continued. Richard led the way since he said that he could see the singer. Richard whispered. "There, see the red hat bobbing between the furze and the catkins". James followed although he could not see anything. After several minutes zigzagging, Richard stopped. They had reached the end of the trees and could see the old castle from which the nearby village had got its name. Although they could not see the 'lucky' man, there draped across the last tree were a red hat and a small green jacket. "I was right", said Richard. "I did see a red hat".

"Nobody said you didn't", replied James. "But who is singing and why can't I see him"?

Suddenly the singing stopped and a lilting voice replied. "Look around you and be observant as all children your age should be". Both looked around but still could see nobody. "Are those your clothes"? asked Richard.
"Those are mine", replied the voice.
"But where are you and what's your name"? asked Richard.
"I'm called Lucky and I am in the sky", came the reply. With that both James and Richard looked upwards. There sitting on a rainbow was Lucky, a man with a dark pointed beard and black hair scraped back in a pony-tail. He had a white open-necked shirt, a gold belt and yellow velvet trousers. His shoes gleamed as if they were solid gold. In his hand he held a small can of gold coins.

James was speechless. Where did Lucky come from and how did he get gold shoes and gold coins?
"I know what you are thinking James" said Lucky as he shifted the can from his right to his left hand. "Well, I usually live over there", said he as he indicated the old castle, "but on work days when I dig for gold, I cool off by sitting on a rainbow".
"Can anyone dig for gold"? asked James.
"Anyone can dig but only a few will find it. To discover gold you need to be observant. You and Richard need to look around you more and see the beauty of nature. Now that's real gold"! With that he was gone, vanishing into the back of a cloud with a flourish. James turned to Richard. "What do you make of that"? he asked. "I don't know" said Richard "But from now on I for one will keep my eyes open and take

Lucky's advice to become more observant. My dad often says that the beauty of the environment is more valuable than money because once lost it cannot be replaced. I think that Lucky was telling us that we should look after it". James nodded. "Let's pick up all the papers and bottles. Imagine how nice the castle could be if we clean it up". The rainbow disappeared and the sun shone on Castletown.

TOM, WOLFIE AND THE DUKE

Tom and Wolfie his Irish wolfhound lived with Tom's mum and dad in a farmhouse surrounded by a large meadow-like garden. William his dad had a few acres of land where he kept some cows, pigs, chickens, a donkey and a variety of dogs. William was a kind man. He always stressed the importance of treating the animals well and built a large barn to store hay and to shelter the animals in cold weather.

Tom and Wolfie were inseparable. The pair usually went walking during the day. Recently however Tom noticed that Wolfie crept out through the back gate for up to an hour at night. Tom had been unable to follow him because his mum Mary told him not to do so. He was worried in case Wolfie got lost but he was reassured when his dad told him that Wolfie usually went into the big barn behind the house just to see his animal friends. "Wolfie needs to talk to the pigs, the cows, the chickens and the other dogs", said William. Tom accepted this explanation however he suspected that Wolfie's recent night roaming was linked to a new arrival at the farm. Tom had seen Wolfie playing with Duke the pig who had been bought from a neighbouring farmer. According to the farmer, Duke was a pig "with attitude".

Wolfie liked Duke's independence and secretly admired him. He liked going to the barn at night because all the animals had a good chat about their lives. Wolfie often felt that he himself had a split personality. One half of him wanted to be obedient to Tom and stay in at night while the other half sometimes overpowered him and made him adventurous and independent. Although generally he was happy with his food which consisted of vegetables, pasta and white meat, on other occasions he felt envious when the family tucked into something called steak and chips. Wolfie also felt that his living quarters were not great. He did have a wooden structure for a bed but it was too hard and even when he signalled to Tom about this he had only been given a small cushion and a mat quite unlike the nice soft duvet he had seen in Tom's room. He did have the run of the house and garden which he liked but he intended to show Tom that he would like a soft bed. He would not shred that duvet. Instead he would roll it up and drag it into his living quarters in the garage!

One morning as Tom finished his breakfast and got ready to go to school, he spoke as usual to Wolfie. "Guard the family, house and garden while I am away. See you later. We will go for a long walk when I come back". Wolfie barked to let Tom know that he understood what was required of him and off

Tom went. In fact Wolfie was going to a meeting in the barn organised by Duke however he would still be able to keep an eye on Mary and William, the house and the garden. By the time that Tom left Wolfie was already late for the barn meeting.

The barn door was pushed shut when Wolfie finally got there. Usually he could open doors as his nose was very strong however the barn door was heavy. He could hear a lot of noise inside. He was able to make out the sound of Duke and the other pigs as they were squealing for attention. He heard Pete the labrador barking furiously and Sissy the miniature poodle shouting in unison. The chickens were crowing and Daisy the head cow was mooing as if trying to calm the situation. Wolfie was unable to get in! He sat by the door for what must have been a long time because he eventually heard Tom calling him. Tom approached the barn and found Wolfie sitting dolefully outside the barn door. He soon understood that Wolfie wanted to go in so he pushed the door open and both of them entered the barn.

Tom could not believe his eyes. Inside, a group of dogs were playing snooker. There was a labrador leaning against an old table. On the far side a large grey collie dog with the face of a pirate was hitting the ball wildly with a long brush instead of a cue. Sitting on the table gesticulating furiously was a poodle. There were several other dogs present. All were enjoying themselves. In the opposite corner there was a group of chickens. Their faces were huddled together as if there was some wonderful subject of conversation.

Tom noticed that Wolfie had moved swiftly to the middle

of the barn where Duke a large pig was surrounded by other pigs, three cows and a donkey. The donkey was eating a bunch of carrots. Suddenly the big pig saw them both. "Come on in", he said. "We are having a meeting of the farm animals but you Tom are welcome to join us. Wolfie says that you are a kind master".

Tom noticed that other animals were present including several ducks, an owl and a few bats hanging out of the rafters. At the very back and merging with the hay a small fox listened intently as his eyes darted from the chickens to the ducks, however he was wary of the big black cat that in turn was eyeing both the fox and the bats. All the animals seemed to be waiting for a meeting to start. Most were looking in Duke's direction who said. "Animals and Tom, welcome to the meeting".

Duke went on to explain the purpose of the meeting which was to get rights for all animals including all fish species. After clearing his throat and drinking water from a wall siphon, he began. "Thanks to recent studies on our cousins the apes and on fish, the intelligence of animals is evident for all to see. It is time for us to have rights. Animals often suffer both physical and mental abuse and this is usually caused by uneducated and greedy humans. We now realize that some humans tend to treat animals badly because they think that animals do not feel pain. Our first aim is to tell everyone that animals feel pain just like humans. Humans need to be educated. As you know animals are often killed and eaten. Some humans have almost wiped out some of our animal cousins. As if that was not bad enough, some animals are cruelly killed while their friends unable to help them, look

46

on. All this is not acceptable. Animals are not put on this earth to be mistreated. After all that animals do for humans, they must be treated with respect".

Wolfie was spellbound. So was Tom. Duke was saying things they had always wanted to say. Duke had style, and human guile! His eyes were intelligent and kept moving around the room. Suddenly Duke spoke to Tom. "What do you think"? he asked.

"I agree with all that you have said", replied Tom calmly, as he found that he had no fear amongst his new-found friends in the barn. "What's more", he added. "I think that all those fighting matches between bears, dogs, hens and cocks which humans artificially arrange, have got to be stopped".

"Good point", said Duke.

"Hear, hear" added a chorus from all the animals in the barn.

Suddenly a blue-grey parrot jumped onto a chair. "But how do we stop those revolting set-up matches"? she asked in a lilting tone.

"We must talk to people in authority", said Duke nodding at the parrot. A few minutes later as the parrot now assumed centre-stage to discuss further problems, the Duke sidled up to Tom and Wolfie who were both trembling but this time with excitement! Duke looked at Tom. "Do you know anybody with influence"? he asked. Tom was flattered and quickly replied. "Yes, my school teacher is quite influential and in fact he is a member of the Humane Society".

"He will do for a start, anyhow", replied the Duke. Wolfie drew himself up to his full height and looked admiringly at Tom. Tom had already begun to prepare a bill of rights for all animals.

"Tom, Tom wake up". His mum Mary was standing over him. "That bill of rights you've been shouting about will have to be completed after school"!

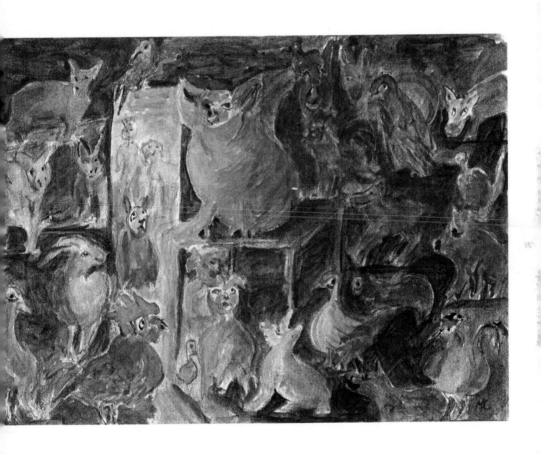

Lightning Source UK Ltd.
Milton Keynes UK
02 March 2010

150833UK00001B/19/P